Edgar Allan Poe's

The Fall of the House of Usher

Adapted by David E. Cutts

Illustrated by Bert Dodson

TROLL ASSOCIATES

Library of Congress Cataloging in Publication Data

Cutts, David.
   Edgar Allan Poe's The fall of the House of
Usher.

   Summary: A visitor to a gloomy mansion finds
a childhood friend dying under the spell of a
family curse.
   [1. Horror—Fiction] I. Dodson, Bert, ill.
II. Poe, Edgar Allan, 1809-1849. Fall
of the House of Usher. III. Title. IV. Title:
Fall of the House of Usher.
PZ7.C996Ecg   [Fic]   81-15958
ISBN 0-89375-624-5   AACR2
ISBN 0-89375-625-3 (pbk.)

Printed in the United States of America
10 9 8 7 6 5 4 3 2 1

One dark autumn day, when the clouds hung low in the sky, I rode on horseback through the dreary countryside. By evening, I could see the melancholy House of Usher. With the first glimpse of that bleak and lonely building, a sense of gloom overcame me.

What was it that chilled me so? I gazed at the reflection of the scene in the black lake that lay nearby. But the reflection in the still waters made me shudder even more.

I planned to stay in this gloomy mansion for some time. Roderick Usher, the owner of the house, was ill. He had written, asking me to come, and I had agreed. As boys, we had been close friends, but I had not seen him for years. I knew little of my friend, except that he came from a very old family.

As I looked up from the reflection in the lake, I thought I saw a strange fog about the house. But I shook off what must have been a dream and looked straight at the building. It was very old and discolored. A tangled web of mold clung to the roof.

None of the walls had fallen, although many of the stones were crumbling badly. Still, only a careful observer would have seen the single crack that zig-zagged down the wall, from the roof to the dark waters of the lake. I rode over a short bridge to the house, where a servant took my horse.

Inside, another servant led me through dark and winding halls. Many of the ordinary objects I saw stirred vague feelings of dread in me. On one of the staircases, I passed the family doctor. He looked at me, his face full of suspicion, and said not one word. The servant threw open a door and took me into a dimly lighted room.

Dark draperies hung upon the walls, and many books and musical instruments lay scattered about. An air of deep gloom hung over all. Usher rose and greeted me, and I was astonished at how much he had changed. His face was pale as death. His uncombed hair floated wildly about his face.

He told me that his illness was a family curse, for which there was no cure. His senses had grown so sharp that all but the softest lights and sounds, and all but the mildest odors and tastes filled him with horror.

"I am slave to a strange terror," he said. "When I die, it will surely be in a struggle with that grim ghost called FEAR."

His sister, the lady Madeline, had long suffered from a strange illness. At such times, her entire body became rigid, and she would not respond to anything. Soon after my arrival, I caught a glimpse of her. I later learned that her condition had worsened.

For several days, the lady Madeline was sick in bed. I tried to lift Roderick Usher's spirits. We painted and read together, and I listened to his wild playing on the guitar. As I grew to know him better, I realized that nothing would ever cheer him. Darkness and gloom seemed to pour from him.

Usher believed that the decaying trees, the overgrown mold, and even the crumbling stones of the mansion walls, had caused a strange condition to form about the house. He thought that this condition had affected the lives of his ancestors, and had made him what he was.

One evening, Usher suddenly told me that the lady Madeline was dead. Before her burial, he wanted to put her corpse in the cellar of the house. I helped him place the body in the coffin. Then we carried it down to a dark, damp room, directly beneath my bedroom.

We passed through a long hall, then through a heavy iron door that made a sharp grating sound as it moved on its hinges. We placed the coffin upon a table and opened the lid. The disease had left a faint blush upon lady Madeline's face. A small smile was on her lips. We screwed down the lid, locked the door, and returned upstairs.

15

After several days of grief, I saw a change in my friend. His usual manner disappeared. He roamed from room to room hurriedly. His color was even paler than before. His voice trembled, as if in terror. At times, I thought he was trying to tell me some terrible secret.

At other times, I thought perhaps Roderick Usher was mad. For hours on end, he would gaze into emptiness, all the while listening to some imaginary sound. It was no wonder, then, that his condition terrified me. I felt the effects of his behavior slowly but surely creeping upon me.

These feelings grew even stronger about seven or eight days after the lady Madeline had been placed in the cellar. I had gone to bed, but could not sleep. I tried to blame my nervousness on my surroundings—perhaps it was the gloomy furniture, or the dark and tattered draperies in the room.

I began to shake. I sat up and looked into the darkness. Low sounds reached my ears. Where they came from I could not tell. Rising, I threw on my clothes and began pacing to and fro. A storm was building outside, and great gusts of wind blew against my window.

Suddenly, I heard a footstep on the stairs outside my room. A knock on the door followed. Usher entered, carrying a lamp. His look was one of madness. He stared about in silence, and then he said, "And you have not seen it?—But stay! You shall!" Then he threw open the window to the storm.

The fury of a gust of wind nearly lifted us from our feet. Thick clouds hung low over the house, blacking out the moon and stars. There was no lightning, yet everything glowed with an unnatural light. A faintly glowing fog hung about the mansion like a shroud.

I quickly closed the window. "Come, let me read to you," I said, picking up a book. The book was called the *Mad Trist*. Usher listened with interest to the part of the tale where the hero breaks into the house of a hermit. I read: "Ethelred brought his club down upon the door. Then he cracked and ripped the plankings, and the noise of splintering wood echoed throughout the forest."

I paused. From some faraway part of the mansion, there came a faint cracking and ripping sound—an echo of the very sound I had just read about. It was this coincidence alone that caught my attention, for on a stormy night like this, such a sound was not unusual.

I continued reading. "Ethelred entered, but saw no sign of the hermit. Instead, he found a huge scaly dragon with fiery tongue, guarding a shield of shining brass. The brave knight brought his club down hard. The dragon fell before him, letting out a shriek so horrid and harsh that Ethelred had to cover his ears against the dreadful noise."

24

I paused again, for now I *did* hear a distant sound. It was a harsh screaming or grating—and it was exactly what I had imagined the dragon's shriek would be. I was terrified. Still, I tried not to excite my friend, for I was not certain that he had heard the sounds.

Usher had moved his chair, so that he now faced the door. His head had dropped upon his chest, but he was not asleep. His eyes were wide open, and his lips were trembling. He rocked from side to side with a gentle swaying movement.

I returned to the book, and read, "Now Ethelred vowed he
would have the shield, so he pulled the dragon's body aside,
and strode closer. But the shield fell to the floor with a mighty
and terrible ringing sound." As I read these words, I heard a
hollow, metallic echo—just as if a shield of brass had fallen
heavily upon the floor!

I leaped to my feet, but Usher continued rocking. A sickly smile quivered on his lips. He spoke in a hurried murmur. "Now hear it? Yes, I hear it, and *have* heard it, long—many minutes, many hours, many days. Yet I *dared* not speak. *We have put her living in the tomb!*

"Did I not say that my senses were sharp? I heard her first weak movements in the coffin many days ago, yet I dared not speak. Oh! She comes! I have heard her footsteps on the stair!" He sprang to his feet crying, *"Madman! I tell you that she now stands outside the door!"*

At that very moment, the door opened. And there stood the figure of the lady Madeline of Usher. There was blood upon her white robes. She had clearly been through a terrible struggle. For a moment, she swayed outside the door and then fell in, upon her brother. Together they fell to the floor. They were dead.

From that room, and from that mansion, I fled. The storm raged as I crossed the land bridge, and a light shone along the path. I turned to see where it was coming from, for there was nothing behind me but the house and its shadows.

The light was from the full, blood-red moon. It shone through that zig-zag crack in the wall. As I watched, the crack quickly widened—the storm raged—and I saw the walls cave in. And then I heard the roar of rushing water as the dark lake flooded over the rubble of the *House of Usher.*